DADDY, COULD I HAVE AN ELEPHANT?

BY
JAKE WOLF

Pictures by
MARYLIN HAFNER

GREENWILLOW BOOKS NEW YORK

This book is a presentation of Atlas Editions, Inc.
For information about Atlas Editions book clubs
for children write to: **Atlas Editions, Inc.,**
4343 Equity Drive, Columbus, Ohio 43228.

Published by arrangement with Greenwillow Books, a
division of William Morrow & Company, Inc.
Weekly Reader is a federally registered trademark
of Weekly Reader Corporation.

1998 edition

Watercolors, colored pencils, and pen and ink were used
for the full-color art. The text type is Della Robbia BT.
Text copyright © 1996 by Jake Wolf
Illustrations copyright © 1996 by Marylin Hafner

First Edition 10 9 8 7 6 5 4 3 2 1

LIBRARY OF CONGRESS CATALOGING-IN-PUBLICATION DATA

Wolf, Jake.
Daddy, could I have an elephant? / by Jake Wolf ; pictures by Marylin Hafner.
 p.   cm.
Summary: Despite his father's objections, Tony insists on wanting such
impractical pets as an elephant, a python, or a flamingo.
ISBN 0-688-13294-4 (trade).   ISBN 0-688-13295-2 (lib. bdg.)
[1. Animals—Fiction.   2. Pets—Fiction.]   I. Hafner, Marylin, ill.   II. Title.
PZ7.W81913Dad   1996   [E]—dc20   94-27168   CIP   AC

For Jerry
—J. W.

For Susan and friends
—M. H.

"Daddy," said Tony. "I need a pet."

"You do?" said his father.

"Yes," said Tony.

"What kind?" said his father.
"Could I have an elephant?"
said Tony.

"An elephant?" said his father.
"Where would you keep it?"
"Here in the apartment," said Tony.
"How would you feed it? Where
would it drink?"
"It could drink out of the bathtub,"
said Tony. "We could send out
for Chinese."

"What if it got lonely?" said his father.
"Elephants live in herds."

"We could get another elephant
to keep it company," said Tony.

"How would we move the elephants up here to the third floor?" said his father. "Like pianos," said Tony. "Pull them on ropes."

"I don't think elephants would fit
   through the window," said his father.
"We could try," said Tony.
"What if they got stuck?" said his father.
"People would talk about us."
"What would they say?" said Tony.
"They'd say we're that family with the
   elephants sticking out the windows."

"Well, how about a pony?" said Tony.
"A pony could walk up the stairs."
"What would you do with it?" said
his father.
"I'd gallop around the apartment and
jump over the furniture," said Tony.
"It would leave hoof marks," said
his father.

"I'd like to have a python,"
said Tony. "Twenty feet long."
"Where would you keep it?"
said his father.
"Some of it on the sofa," said Tony,
"the rest of it on chairs."

"Where would *we* sit?" said his father.

"A flock of woolly sheep would be nice," said Tony. "They could keep us warm at night."

"Sheep go *B-A-A-A* when you're trying to sleep," said his father.
"Not if they're asleep, too," said Tony. "We could give them a definite bedtime."
"What if they woke up early?" said his father.

"Gorillas would be fun," said Tony.
"They could go out the window and climb up and down the side of the building."
"What if they decided to climb in somebody else's window?" said his father.

SEE YA LATER, TONY.

"A parrot would be a good pet,"
said Tony. "Somebody to talk to."
"Parrots screech," said his father.

"What about a quiet bird?" said Tony.
"I'd like a flamingo, and maybe a pelican."
"Flamingos and pelicans like beaches,"
 said his father.

"We could put sand in my room, and a palm tree," said Tony. "Flamingos and pelicans need to be warm," said his father.

"We could close all the windows
and turn up the heat," said Tony.
"Expensive," said his father.

"I know what," said Tony.
"What?" said his father.
"We could fill the living room
 with water."
"And then?" said his father.
"We could get a dolphin,"
 said Tony, "and a baby whale."
"Both?" said his father.

"All the kids from school could come over and swim with the dolphin and the baby whale," said Tony. "Then they could sit on the sand under the palm tree and have a picnic."

His father didn't say anything.
"I'd make the sandwiches," said Tony.
"I'd clean up afterward."

Tony and his father were quiet for a while.
"Maybe we should get something small,"
said Tony.
"What could that be?" said his father.
"Puppies are small," said Tony.
"Just what I was thinking," said his father.
"Puppies are small."

"Could we get one?" said Tony.
"Maybe we could take a look this
 afternoon," said his father.
"What about this morning?" said Tony.
"It's possible," said his father.
"What about now?" said Tony.
"Now is good," said his father, and they
 went out the door.